Jane Hissey
JOLLY TALL

RED FOX

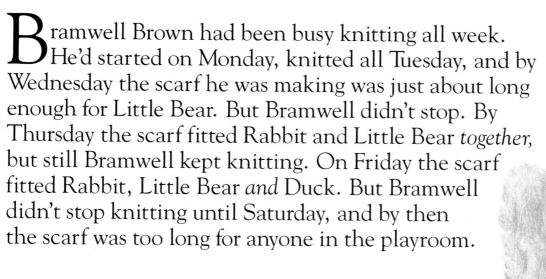

Bramwell Brown had been busy knitting all week. He'd started on Monday, knitted all Tuesday, and by Wednesday the scarf he was making was just about long enough for Little Bear. But Bramwell didn't stop. By Thursday the scarf fitted Rabbit and Little Bear *together*, but still Bramwell kept knitting. On Friday the scarf fitted Rabbit, Little Bear *and* Duck. But Bramwell didn't stop knitting until Saturday, and by then the scarf was too long for anyone in the playroom.

'I suppose we could cut it up,' said Little Bear. 'Then everyone would have a scarf.'

'It would all come unknitted then,' said Old Bear.

Little Bear tried on the scarf once more, but he tripped over the end and landed upside down in Bramwell's lap. 'Why did you make it so long?' he asked.

'Because people kept interrupting me,' said Bramwell, 'and I forgot to measure it.'

'Never mind,' said Old Bear. 'I'm sure it will come in useful sometime.'

'As a skipping-rope perhaps,' grumbled Duck.

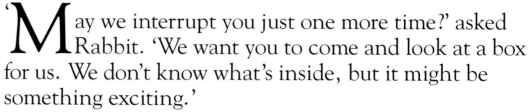

'May we interrupt you just one more time?' asked Rabbit. 'We want you to come and look at a box for us. We don't know what's inside, but it might be something exciting.'

'Like treasure,' said Little Bear.

'Probably empty,' muttered Duck. Rabbit led the toys to a tall box tied up with string. Bramwell walked all round it.

'It hasn't got a label,' he said. 'I'll make a hole in it and look inside.' With his knitting needle Bramwell poked a tiny hole in the box.

The box said 'Ouch!'

'Can boxes talk?' whispered Rabbit.

'Well this one just did,' said Little Bear.

'It wasn't the box,' said Old Bear. 'It was the something inside.'

'What a pity,' said Little Bear. 'It can't be treasure then.'

'Well it might be something *guarding* the treasure,' said Rabbit hopefully. 'Go on Bramwell, open it — please.'

Bramwell studied the mysterious package. 'I think I ought to talk to it first and see if it's friendly.' He crept over to the little hole. 'Hello,' he called softly. 'Are you friend or foe?'

'Hello,' came the muffled reply. 'I think I must be a friend because I haven't heard of a foe, unless a foe is better than a friend in which case I'm one of those.'

'It doesn't sound very sure,' said Duck.

'I think we ought to be prepared anyway,' said Rabbit. 'I'll find a net to catch it in, in case it suddenly jumps out.'

Duck fetched a rope to tie it up. 'It might escape from your net,' he said. Little Bear found a bag to put the treasure in, just in case there was some.

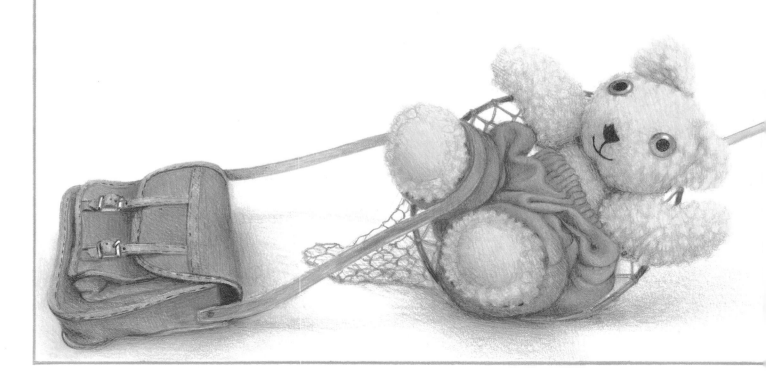

Very carefully, Bramwell and Old Bear untied the string and lifted the lid.

They all held their breath . . .

Two little furry horns appeared first, then two large furry ears, and then a great big friendly furry face.

'Oh that's better,' said the something, smiling down at the toys. 'Hello everyone, what have you got there?'

Rabbit and Duck quickly dropped the net and the rope, but Little Bear clung hopefully to his bag.

'Excuse me,' he said, 'are you standing on some treasure?'

The big furry head disappeared into the box and then popped out again. 'Sorry,' it said, 'there's no treasure in here.'

'What are you standing on then?' asked Rabbit.

'Just the bottom of the box,' it replied.

'Gosh!' gasped Little Bear. 'You must be jolly tall.'

'That's right,' said their new friend. 'I'm Jolly Tall, that's my name, but you can call me Jolly if you like. Do you like my house?'

'Well actually,' said Little Bear, 'we thought it was just a box. It would look better with doors and windows.'

Jolly agreed, so the toys set to work. Little Bear cut out the windows and doors, Bramwell fetched some material for the curtains, and Rabbit fixed them in place with glue and pins. All the toys helped, and were very pleased when at last the box looked like a real house. Little Bear went in to tell Jolly that it was ready. 'You can come out now,' he said.

'I'm afraid I can't,' said Jolly. 'I'm too tall for the front door.'

'You could *jump* out,' suggested Rabbit.

Jolly jumped, but he couldn't get anywhere near high enough. Little Bear rushed out of the door very quickly; a jumping Jolly seemed more dangerous than a still one.

'Fetch the crane!' said Old Bear. 'We'll *lift* you out.'

'Will that mean going up?' asked Jolly nervously.

'Of course,' said Old Bear. 'Up and over the top of the box.'

'But I don't like heights,' said Jolly. 'My head seems to think it's high enough as it is.'

'I know what to do,' said Little Bear, 'I'll put my paws over your eyes. Then you won't see how high you're going.'

Puffing and panting, the toys managed to lift the crane up on to a pile of books to make it taller than Jolly Tall. Little Bear tied the chain to a handkerchief around Jolly's middle, climbed up Jolly's neck, and leaned over to cover his eyes with his paws.

'We're ready,' he shouted, and Bramwell began to turn the handle of the crane.

Very slowly, Jolly began to rise out of the box, and soon the toys could see nearly all of his long neck. Feeling very excited, Bramwell wound the handle around faster and faster as more and more of Jolly appeared.

'We're up,' cried Little Bear, taking one paw off Jolly's eye to wave to the others.

Then it happened . . . .

J olly saw how high up he was and began to wave his legs about like a windmill — the box wobbled, Jolly wobbled, and both went crashing to the floor. Little Bear flew across the room and disappeared. But nobody noticed; they were too busy pulling Jolly out of his box.

The toys helped Jolly up and on to his feet again.

'But where's Little Bear?' they asked, anxiously peering into the battered box.

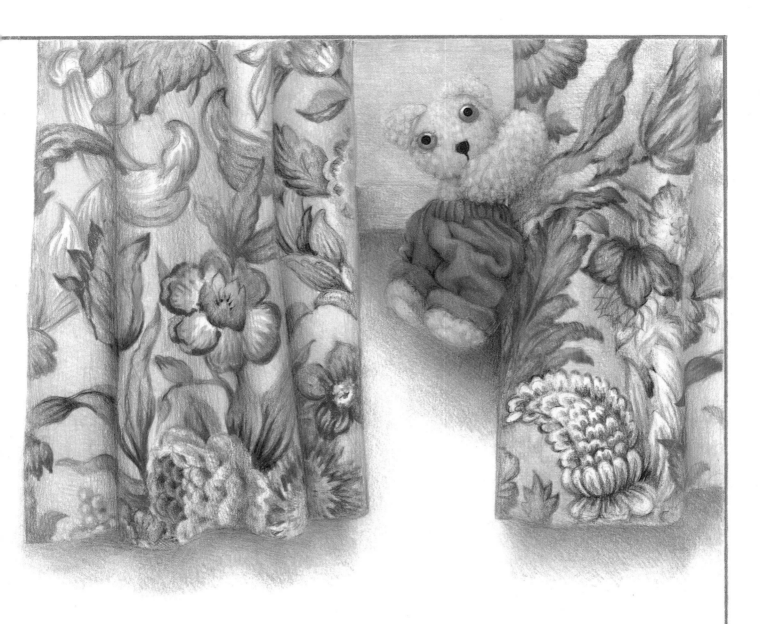

'I'm here,' came a little voice from across the room. 'I flew.' There was Little Bear, clinging to the playroom curtain by the tips of his paws. 'Help!' he shouted. 'I can't get down.'

'Hang on,' said Jolly, galloping to the rescue. 'I think I can get you down. You can slide down my neck.'

Little Bear could hang on no longer. He let go of the curtain, shot all the way down Jolly's neck and fell, plop, into the net that Bramwell held out for him. He enjoyed it so much that he wanted another go, but Old Bear said it was time for bed.

'Where's Jolly going to sleep?' asked Rabbit.
'I'll swap my bed for your house, Jolly,' said Little Bear.

'You can *have* my house,' said Jolly cheerfully. 'Giraffes sleep standing up; just a blanket would do for me.'

Rabbit and Little Bear found a nice cosy blanket for their new friend. But they couldn't get all of him under it. 'Your neck's going to get cold,' sighed Little Bear.

Bramwell looked at Jolly with his neck sticking out of the blanket.

'Just a moment,' he cried rushing off. A few minutes later he returned with a carefully wrapped parcel.

'It's a present for you, Jolly,' he said. 'A *welcome* present.'

Jolly unwrapped the parcel. Inside was the very, very long red scarf. 'It's lovely,' he said. 'It's the best welcome present ever. But how did you know I'd need it?'

'We knew *someone* would,' said Bramwell, and he wound the extra long scarf round and round and round Jolly's long neck.

'We thought you were a box of treasure this morning,' said Rabbit.

'Or just an empty box,' said Duck.

'But we're very glad you weren't,' said Little Bear. 'A new friend is much more fun than a whole boxful of treasure!'

For Harriet and Russell

A Red Fox Book

Published by Random Century Children's Books
20 Vauxhall Bridge Road, London SW1V 2SA

A division of the Random Century Group
London Melbourne Sydney Auckland
Johannesburg and agencies throughout the world

First published by Hutchinson Children's Books 1990

Red Fox edition 1992

Printed in Hong Kong

ISBN 0 09 962480 X